Harry, the Little Hare

Lilo Fromm

J.M. Dent & Sons Limited
London   Melbourne   Toronto

There was once upon a time
a large family of hares.

One fine morning,
Harry – the oldest of seven –
decided to go in search of adventure.
'Harry,' said his mother, 'be careful,
and make sure you are back
in time for supper.'
'Yes, Mummy,' said Harry,
who always did his best to be good.

Waving goodbye to his mother
and six brothers and sisters,
Harry bounded off across the fields,
his nose in the air
sniffing for adventure.
Unfortunately he was so busy
sniffing the air for adventure
that he didn't see the stream
in front of him.

'Watch out, you silly young hare!'
cried a passing dragonfly.

But the warning came too late,
and before he knew what was happening,
Harry had tumbled head over heels
into the stream. Splash!

'Help!' he shouted as he fell,
but only the startled fishes heard his cry.

Swiftly the current carried
Harry downstream.
At first the little hare was frightened.

'Adventures are all very well,'
he thought to himself,
'but they are so much better
when they are dry.'

He tried floating on his back,
he tried swimming on his front . . .
A large red squirrel watched
in amazement as Harry went past.
He'd never seen a swimming hare before.
Just as Harry thought he could
paddle no longer . . .

. . . he saw ahead of him an old mill,
its huge waterwheel turning
as it ground the flour.

Quickly Harry grabbed hold of the wheel and was lifted smoothly out of the stream, water splashing all around him.

As the wheel turned,
so Harry rose higher.

'Jump now!' cried a handsome butterfly,
trying to be helpful.
And Harry did just that.
With one leap he was on the grass,
shaken, soaked, but happy.

'What an exciting adventure
I've had today!'
thought the little hare.
'And won't Mummy be surprised
to hear I've been swimming . . .'
Then, remembering his promise
to be back in time for supper,
Harry set off for home
as fast as his little legs would carry him.

It was dark when he arrived;
the moon and the stars
were shining brightly.
Harry's mother and brothers and sisters
welcomed him home with cries of joy.

'Oh, how worried we were!'
exclaimed his mother,
lifting Harry up and shaking him
until his coat was dry.
'But what a brave little hare you are!'

That night, tucked up in bed,
Harry dreamed of his splendid day,
as well as of the adventures
he hoped to have.
Only next time, he would make sure
he stayed *dry*.